A FAMILY FOR FARU

ANITHA RAO-ROBINSON

Illustrations by

KAREN PATKAU

pajamapress

First published in Canada and the United States in 2020

Text copyright © 2020 Anitha Rao-Robinson
Illustration copyright © 2020 Karen Patkau
This edition copyright © 2020 Pajama Press Inc.
This is a first edition.

10 9 8 7 6 5 4 3 2 1

www.pajamapress.ca   info@pajamapress.ca

 Canada Council   Conseil des arts   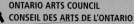 ONTARIO ARTS COUNCIL   Canadä
for the Arts   du Canada   CONSEIL DES ARTS DE L'ONTARIO
                                                   an Ontario government agency
                                                   un organisme du gouvernement de l'Ontario

The publisher gratefully acknowledges the support of the Canada Council for the Arts and the
Ontario Arts Council for its publishing program. We acknowledge the financial support of the
Government of Canada through the Canada Book Fund (CBF) for our publishing activities.

Library and Archives Canada Cataloguing in Publication

Title: A family for Faru / Anitha Rao-Robinson ; illustrations by Karen Patkau.
Names: Rao-Robinson, Anitha, author. | Patkau, Karen, illustrator.
Identifiers: Canadiana 20200198297 | ISBN 9781772780963 (hardcover)
Classification: LCC PS8635.A62 F36 2020 | DDC jC813/.6—dc23

Publisher Cataloging-in-Publication Data (U.S.)

Names: Rao-Robinson, Anitha, author. | Patkau, Karen, illustrator.
Title: A Family for Faru / Anitha Rao-Robinson ; illustrations by Karen Patkau.
Description: Toronto, Ontario Canada : Pajama Press, 2020. | Summary: "Tetenya is looking for a family of rhinos to
take in an orphan named Faru, but he can see poachers nearby. He stains Faru's horn pink with berry juice, making
it useless to the poachers. At last they find a herd protected by a ranger, and Faru is safe"— Provided by publisher.
Identifiers: ISBN 978-1-77278-096-3 (hardback)
Subjects: LCSH: Rhinoceroses-- Juvenile fiction. | Poaching -- Juvenile fiction. | Adoption
– Juvenile fiction. | BISAC: JUVENILE FICTION / Animals / Hippos & Rhinos. | JUVENILE
FICTION / Science & Nature / Environment. | JUVENILE FICTION / Family / Adoption.
Classification: LCC PZ7.R367Fam |DDC [F] – dc23

Original art created with digital media
Cover and book design by Rebecca Bender

Manufactured by Qualibre Inc./Print Plus
Printed in China

Pajama Press Inc.
181 Carlaw Ave. Suite 251 Toronto, Ontario Canada, M4M 2S1

Distributed in Canada by UTP Distribution
5201 Dufferin Street Toronto, Ontario Canada, M3H 5T8

Distributed in the U.S. by Ingram Publisher Services
1 Ingram Blvd. La Vergne, TN 37086, USA

For all the rhinos like Faru,
I hope someday soon you live your lives in peace and
quiet, wild and free. You deserve that and so much more.
—A.R.

For Nicola and Hannah
—K.P.

THE SUN creeps above the treetops and warms the air with the smell of lemongrass. Tetenya inhales the tangy scent.

MMMM! MMMM! MMMM!

Beside him, Faru rubs against a tree. Tetenya scratches the orphan rhino's back. "I know it has been days since we came upon you all alone. Mama's been trying to find you a new family."

Tetenya looks out across the stream. "Maybe it's time I tried instead."

"Tetenya," Mama calls. "Bring me some water berries, please. Tetenya pulls off handfuls of berries, offers some to Faru, and puts the rest in his basket for his mother.

He dashes back to his house. Too fast!
The basket of berries slips from Tetenya's arms.

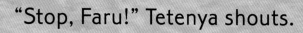

"Stop, Faru!" Tetenya shouts.

BA-DOOM

BA-DOOM

BA-DOOM

Faru doesn't stop. He gallops forward.

STOMPING!

CRUSHING!

SQUISHING!

Staining his feet pink.

"That was our lunch," Tetenya scolds. The little rhino lowers his head.

Mama smiles. "It's all right. You can pick more berries later."

Faru runs in circles, kicking up dust. "Come on," Tetenya says to Faru. "Let's go find some rhinos!"

And they set off.

They pass giraffes gliding through the long grass.
But no rhinos.

SWISH

SWISH

SWISH

They dash by a troop of vervet monkeys snacking high in the trees. But no rhinos.

SLURP
SLURP
SLURP

SCRITCH   SCRITCH   SCRITCH

They weave around a family of guinea fowl scrounging for seeds. Still no rhinos.

They climb a hill. The entire savannah spreads out below in greens, golds, and browns.

Faru raises his head and squeals.

EEEEE

EEEEE EEEEE

No rhinos answer his call.

"Don't worry. We'll find them."
Tetenya rubs Faru's horn. "But the
air is so hot. Let's rest for a bit."

They cool off in a pond of mud…

...gather more water berries for lunch...

...and fall asleep under the
shade of a jackalberry tree.

The sound of cracking twigs wakes them. They peek around the tree.

Hunters.

Faru hides his face in the tree's roots.

"We are brothers now," Tetenya says. "I will keep you safe."

But how? Tetenya thumps his frustration into the ground. Leftover berries ooze between his toes, staining them pink.

A wild idea forms in his head.

Tetenya straightens just as
the two men appear.
One steps forward.

"Who did this to the rhino's
horn?" he demands.

Tetenya hides his hands
behind his back. Faru
nuzzles Tetenya's legs.

The man scowls. "We can't
take one with a horn like
that." And they stomp off.

CLOMP

CLOMP

CLOMP

Tetenya and Faru wait...and wait...and wait.

It's safe," Tetenya says, stroking Faru. "They're far away now."

Faru raises his head and trills his relief.

EEE
EEE
EEE

This time, his joyous cries echo back.

EEEEE

Tetenya and Faru gallop toward the sounds.

At last they come upon a crash of rhinos drinking
from a watering hole. Nearby, a ranger waves.

"I found a baby rhino for you to look after,"
Tetenya calls, waving back. He smiles down
at Faru. "Here is your new family."

The ranger ambles over to Faru and rubs his horn.

The other rhinos lift their heads in welcome.

EEE

EEE

EEE

EEEEE

Faru runs toward the watering hole—

—then stops. He turns back.

"Go on," Tetenya urges.
"I'll see you again soon."

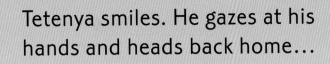

Tetenya smiles. He gazes at his hands and heads back home...

...stopping for some water berries along the way.

RHiNOS

RHiNOS have roamed the earth for millions of years, but now they are an endangered species, hunted for their horns. These are often ground up and used in traditional medicines. At the start of the 1900's, there were approximately 500,000 rhinos in Africa and Asia. Today it is estimated that there are less than 30,000 rhinos left in the wild.

My family and I spent several days on a reserve in South Africa. It took our wildlife tracker a couple of days to locate the rhinos. Part of me hoped the animals were too well hidden to be found, because then poachers might not be able to find them either. Eventually, we did find two gorgeous rhinos. My heart ached at how slowly they moved and how they allowed us to get so close—they were such an easy target for poachers. Though the rhinos were on a reserve, unfortunately, it didn't mean they were safe. Poachers would still trespass on protected land and hunt them.

Thankfully, there are groups trying to save the rhinos. Some are devoted to caring for orphaned rhinos. This is an extremely difficult task, because the young rhinos have been traumatized by the loss of their mothers at the hands of hunters. But with love and a lot of care, many survive. And once the rhinos are older, they venture out into the protected reserve, but they are always under the watchful eye of a ranger. When new orphans like Faru enter a rhino sanctuary, they are at first kept apart from the other rhinos to make sure they are healthy. They are then introduced to their new family one at a time.

There are also some groups that continue to research ways to make the rhino's horn worthless to poachers. One idea is to inject the horn with an eco-friendly, biodegradable dye. The dye cannot be washed away, and is said to be present even when the horn is ground up. Though the dye is safe for both rhinos and other animals in their environment, such as the Ox Pecker, it is not intended for human consumption and can be toxic—thus eliminating the poacher's reason to hunt rhinos. This initiative, though still in the early stages, raised awareness of the plight of rhinos with the appearance of pink-horned rhinos on a variety of social media sites. It was also the inspiration for this story.